Lester counts
his friends

Published by Ray Rourke Publishing Company, Inc.,
Windermere, Florida 32786

Library of Congress Cataloging in Publication Data

Sheehan, Angela.
  Lester counts his friends.

  SUMMARY: A country mouse is introduced to the
numbers 1 through 10 by the residents of his city
cousin's apartment building.
  [1. Counting.   2. Animals—Fiction]
I. Coleman, Jill, joint author.   II. Astrop,
John.   III. Title.
PZ7.S53827Lee   [E]   81-351
ISBN 0-86592-092-3   AACR1

Lester counts his friends

By Angela Sheehan and Jill Coleman

Illustrated by John Astrop

Ray Rourke Publishing Company, Inc.
Windermere, Florida 32786

Lester Squeak was a
little gray mouse.
He lived on his own
under the garden shed.

Sometimes he felt lonely.

"I'm bored," he sighed one morning.

Just then, a letter dropped on to the doormat.

It was from his cousin in the city.
"Come and stay," it said.

"How exciting," thought Lester, and ran to pack his suitcase.

He put on his hat, climbed on his bicycle
and pedaled away.

It was a long, hot ride to town.

His cousin's house seemed very big.
"Town mice must be awfully rich," thought Lester.

But inside, there were apartments. "That's funny," he thought. "The numbers start at the top," so he trudged upstairs.

There was no one about except an old mole, busy at his desk. "No mice here," said the mole. "Try next door."

The two toads next door were no help.
"Sorry young fellow," they croaked.
"Try the crows downstairs."

The three old crows were playing cards.
"We don't like mice," they said. "Shut the door as you go."

All Lester could hear from number four was loud
crunching and munching. He peeped through the mail slot.

"I'll never get an answer from those four pigs," he thought.

Downstairs, five fine foxes were learning to dance.
"I don't know your cousin," said a big red fox,
"but would you care to foxtrot?"
"No," squeaked Lester and scurried away.

In the room next door, six snakes were singing songs. "What a noise," thought Lester, as he slipped away.

Downstairs, he tiptoed past seven snoring badgers, all fast asleep.

Next door, eight parrots squawked and squabbled over their tea. "My cousin wouldn't live with them," thought Lester. "He must be in the last room of all."

But his cousin was not there. Instead, there were
nine squirrels scrubbing, dusting and polishing.
Lester stood in the dust and sighed.
"Oh dear, now I shall have to go all the way back."

He picked up his suitcase and started for home.
Suddenly he heard a noise: "Psst, Lester, over here!"

He had found not only one cousin, but ten.

"Now we can start the party," they cheered. And they did.
Lester laughed and danced and ate all night.

Next morning, all the town mice waved and shouted as Lester set off for home. "Town mice are not so rich after all," though Lester, as he pedaled along. "They live under the floorboards just like me."

Lester's party.

How many moles?

How many toads?

How many crows?

How many snakes?

How many parrots?

How many straws?

How many balloons?

How many crackers?

How many hats?

How many glasses?

Are there more balloons

here . . .

or here?

Are there more balloons

here . . .

or here?

Learning with Lester

*Here are some more ways to use this book to amuse young children
and help them practice simple skills.*

Look at each of the pictures and ask questions such as: "How many drinks are on the toads' table? How many cards are in the crows' hands? How many sheets of music have the snakes got, how many are on the piano, how many on the floor? Are there enough pairs of slippers for the badgers, hats for the toads, cups of tea for the parrots?" Tell the children why the house is No. 55 (that's the total number of animals that live in the house).

Use the book as a starting point for counting games like: "How many chairs, how many windows, how many doors are there? How many legs has a mouse, a dog, a snake, a bee? How many cookies? If you eat one, how many are left? Find three spoons, two mugs, four plates; how many things have you got altogether?"

Encourage the children to talk about Lester. See if they can describe what he is doing in each of the pictures. "Why does he feel bored? Why is he surprised to find the first apartment at the top of the house? Why didn't he stay long at the foxes' apartment or at the parrots'? How did he feel when he couldn't find his cousin's apartment? Why was he pleased that his cousins lived under the floor?" Let the children use their own words.

See if the children can describe the "characters" of the other animals and imitate them. Can they make the noises the animals make; snort or squeal like a pig, hiss like a snake, squawk like a parrot, grunt like a badger, croak like a toad, caw like a crow, and so on. (Don't worry, if you don't know exactly the right sounds yourself.)

Ask the children about colors, too "What color is Lester, his scarf, his case, his cousins? What colors are the other animals? How many squirrels are gray, how many are red?" Go on to ask about other things at home: the cushions, the plates, your clothes, your hair, the plants.

Together, make up another story about a "certain number" of animals (for instance, two cats and a dog or five mice and a bird).

Teach them to sing "Three Blind Mice".